Summer Vacation

By Edith Kunhardt
Illustrated by Kathy Allert

A Golden Book • New York
Western Publishing Company, Inc., Racine, Wisconsin

Copyright © 1986 by Western Publishing Company, Inc. Illustrations copyright © 1986 by Kathy Allert. All rights reserved. Printed in the U.S.A. No part of this book may be reproduced or copied in any form without written permission from the publisher. GOLDEN®, GOLDEN & DESIGN®, A GOLDEN BOOK®, and A LITTLE GOLDEN BOOK® are trademarks of Western Publishing Company, Inc. Library of Congress Catalog Card Number: 83-80021 ISBN 0-307-02045-2/ISBN 0-307-60221-4 (lib. bdg.)
A B C D E F G H I J

Peter and Patrick were friends. They lived next door to each other and went to the same school.

Now it was summer and time for vacation. Patrick was going to the mountains. Peter was going to the seashore.

"Good-by, good-by," they called to each other. "See you in two weeks!"

Patrick and his parents drove and drove until they came to the mountains, where the trees were tall and piny. Their cabin was near a lake.

Every day Patrick and his parents went canoeing and fishing on the lake. One day Patrick caught a sunfish. Another day he caught a trout.

Every day they went swimming. Sometimes Patrick dived off Turtle Rock. Sometimes he put on goggles and looked at the lake bottom.

Every day Patrick took home a smooth stone from the lake shore. One day he found a gray stone with red speckles. "Red is Peter's favorite color," he thought. "I'll save this one for him."

Patrick had a pup tent. His father helped him set it up. Patrick put his sleeping bag and canteen in the tent and pretended he was camping. At bedtime, though, he liked to sleep in his own bed in the cabin.

Every night after supper Patrick lay in his hammock and looked up at the sky through the trees. He thought about the tree house where he and Peter played together at home. He missed Peter, but he knew that they would see each other soon.

On the last day of vacation Patrick and his mom and dad climbed a mountain. Patrick found a stick that helped him climb the steep parts.

At the top of the mountain Patrick and his parents ate
lunch. They picked wild blueberries for dessert.

When it was time to go home Patrick packed his climbing stick and his smooth stones. He thought about Peter at the seashore. He couldn't wait to see him again and tell him all about the mountains and the lake.

At the seashore, Peter had played in the sand every day.
One day he built a sand castle. It was very big, with lots of
tunnels and turrets. He put sticks of driftwood on the turrets
to make them taller.

One piece of driftwood looked like an old man's face.
"This looks like those funny faces Patrick is always drawing,"
Peter thought. "I'll save it for him."

Peter's sister buried him in the sand, all of him except his head. She patted the warm sand down all over him. He lay very still and then let his toes wiggle. When they poked through the sand his sister giggled and tried to cover them up.

Every day Peter and his sister swam in the ocean. Their mom and dad swam too, and lifted them over the big waves.

Sometimes they played a game with the waves. They ran up the sand as a wave washed in, then followed it back to the sea.

Every day Peter took home a new and special sea shell.

One day it rained when they were on the beach. First there were just a few raindrops that made little dimples in the sand. People gathered up their towels and put them under beach umbrellas. When it started to thunder, everyone packed up and went home.

The next day was bright and sunny again. Peter and his mother rode their bicycles to the lighthouse. They climbed the winding staircase and saw the big light that shined at night for the ships at sea. Being up high reminded Peter of Patrick and their tree house.

On the last night of vacation Peter and his family had a picnic on the beach. They built a fire and cooked lobster and corn on the cob. Peter didn't like lobster, so he had a peanut-butter-and-jelly sandwich and corn on the cob. Later everyone toasted marshmallows in the fire.

The next morning Peter packed his sea shells and his piece of driftwood that looked like an old man's face. Vacation was over.

Peter ran over to Patrick's house as soon as he got home. "I brought you some driftwood from the beach," he said.
"And I brought you a red-and-gray stone from the lake," said Patrick.

"Vacation is nice," said Peter, "but I like coming home too."

"I missed our tree house," said Patrick.

"Me too," said Peter. "Want to go out there now?"

"Sure!" said Patrick.

So they did.